ICARUS WAS RIDICULOUS

PAMELA BUTCHART

nosy crow

First published in the UK in 2019 by Nosy Crow Ltd
The Crow's Nest, 14 Baden Place,
London, SE1 1YW, UK

Nosy Crow and associated logos are trademarks and/or registered
trademarks of Nosy Crow Ltd

Published in collaboration with the British Museum

Text copyright © Pamela Butchart, 2019
Cover and illustrations copyright © Thomas Flintham, 2019

The right of Pamela Butchart and Thomas Flintham to be identified
as the author and illustrator respectively of this work has been asserted
by them in accordance with the Copyright, Designs
and Patents Act 1988.

Printed and bound in Great Britain by Clays Ltd, Elcograf S.p.A.

Papers used by Nosy Crow are made from wood grown in
sustainable forests.

ISBN: 978 1 78800 120 5

www.nosycrow.com

The GREEK MYTHS are stories originally told by the Ancient Greeks. They are about GODS AND GODDESSES, who are always meddling in humans' lives, and HEROES and VILLAINS and MONSTERS and WEIRD CREATURES.

There are lots of versions of the stories, but these are IZZY'S.

Contents

Characters in
ICARUS WAS RIDICULOUS,
in order of appearance:

KING MINOS OF CRETE, an odd man
A GARDENER
A COOK
SOME GUARDS
DAEDALUS, an inventor from Athens
ICARUS, his son
THE MINOTAUR, part-man, part-bull
THESEUS, a prisoner
A TOUR GUIDE at the British Museum

One time, our class was in a HOTEL having our BREAKFAST because we were on a SCHOOL TRIP.

And our teacher, Miss Jones, looked

REALLY STRESSED

and she kept counting everyone's HEADS and looking at her WATCH and asking everyone OVER and OVER if they needed to go to the toilet.

So me and Jodi and Maisie all went to the toilet and when we came back Zach was still sitting there and he'd got ANOTHER cup

of tea because it was a HELP YOURSELF BUFFET.

That's when Miss Jones came over and looked at all the TEA CUPS and asked if he needed to go to the toilet and Zach said no. But Miss Jones said that he should GO ANYWAY and that he should go NOW and that we were leaving in EXACTLY SIX MINUTES. So Zach said that he would but then as soon as Miss Jones left he just started drinking his tea again.

I asked Zach if he was going to go to the toilet like Miss Jones said he should and he said he wasn't and that he was going to get another cup of tea instead.

So that's when I said that he was being JUST like ICARUS and that ICARUS never listened to anyone EITHER.

But Zach just stared at me and said, "Who's Icabus?"

So I said that Icabus wasn't anybody but that ICARUS was a boy from ANCIENT GREECE who went to visit CRETE with his dad and never came home because of KING MINOS and all the PIGEON FEATHERS and NOT LISTENING TO PEOPLE.

But Zach said that he still didn't know who I was talking about. So that's when I explained that King Minos of Crete was really HORRIBLE and that when he was just a prince he liked to do things like catch FLIES in bottles and throw MUD PIES in people's windows and cut people's HAIR without asking. And no one ever stood up to

him because they were too scared that he'd shave off their EYEBROWS when they were sleeping because that's what he did to his teacher when he wasn't allowed to write on the board.

Then when Minos became KING he said that he wanted a TOWER built next to his house and that he was going to use it as a PRISON because he thought it would be fun to have some prisoners in a tower because that's just the type of person he was.

As soon as the tower was finished, King Minos was DESPERATE to get his prisoners so he STORMED around the palace looking for someone to do something that ANNOYED him so that he could shout, "RIGHT. That annoyed me so YOU are going to be my first PRISONER!"

But EVERYONE who worked in the palace was on their BEST BEHAVIOUR because they could just TELL that Minos was looking for trouble by his FACE and the way he was WALKING and also because he was wearing his "I'M THE BOSS" T-shirt over his toga which is what he ALWAYS did when he was looking for a fight.

So all of his servants and gardeners and hairdressers tried to stay out of his way and do their best work

EVER.

But then Minos started STARING at everyone and stressing them out and that's when the gardener accidentally cut off one of his FINGERS. And he didn't scream or faint or ANYTHING. He just kept smiling because he didn't want King Minos to get annoyed at him for dripping blood on his daffodils.

But then someone SNEEZED and King Minos WHIPPED his head around, really fast, and shouted, "WHO WAS THAT?!"

Everyone FROZE and didn't say anything and it sort of looked like they were playing MUSICAL STATUES except that people who are playing musical statues don't usually have tears rolling down their faces.

And then someone sneezed AGAIN and King Minos saw that it was his COOK. So that's when Minos said that the first sneeze had annoyed him but that the SECOND

SNEEZE had made him FURIOUS and that the cook was now his prisoner

FOR LIFE.

And Minos was actually really pleased that it had been his cook who did the sneezing because his chips-and-cheese hadn't been CHEESY enough recently.

Then, King Minos pointed to one of his guards and told him to bring him a man called DANDELION because he'd heard that he was the best INVENTOR in all of ANCIENT GREECE.

But the guard just STARED at Minos because he'd never HEARD of a man called

DANDELION before and he wasn't even sure that that was a NAME.

And that's when one of the other guards cleared his throat and said, "Do you mean DAEDALUS, Your Royal Majesty, Highest King of All the World and Universe for Ever and Ever?" (That was what Minos liked to be called.) And King Minos said yes and that he didn't CARE what the man was called and that he just wanted to see him

IMMEDIATELY.

So the guards went and got Daedalus and they had to go quite far actually because Daedalus didn't even live in Crete like they did. He lived in a place called ATHENS.

But when Daedalus finally arrived, King Minos said, "Who's THAT?" because Daedalus had brought his son ICARUS with him and that REALLY ANNOYED King Minos because he knew he was going

to have to let them use his BUNK BEDS
and that was where he liked to keep all his
HEADLESS TEDDIES.

Daedalus gave Icarus a NUDGE because
he was looking down at his sandals and
not speaking to anyone because he was a
TEENAGER.

So Icarus did a really long SIGH and then
he lifted up his head and looked at King
Minos and said, "Hey."

But King Minos didn't say "Hey" back. He
just kept on brushing his hair.

And then he said, "Listen, Dandelion."

So Daedalus looked at the guards to see

if he should correct the king about his name but they just shook their heads really fast so he didn't say anything.

Then Minos said, "I need you to make me a **MAZE** to make sure my prisoners can't escape from my **PRISON** and it better be a **GOOD ONE** or I'll shave off your eyebrows and

And Daedalus gasped because he'd

heard the story about Minos shaving off his teacher's eyebrows but he didn't realise that he'd actually

EATEN THEM TOO!

Minos said that he wanted Daedalus to design him an UNDERGROUND MAZE to go under his HUGE TOWER.

That's when Icarus flicked the hair out of his eyes and said, "What for?"

And King Minos got a WICKED LOOK in his eye and he said, "It's a PRISON. Just a NORMAL prison for my

NORMAL prisoners."

But then he laughed a bit and Icarus looked up at his dad because it was obvious that it WASN'T a normal prison and that King Minos was HIDING SOMETHING.

Then Minos said that it was time for his tea so Daedalus and Icarus went to leave but Minos said, "No. Stay."

So Daedalus and Icarus sat down at the table with King Minos and put napkins on their laps because they thought they were about to get something to eat. But they didn't. So they just had to sit and watch Minos eat his soup.

And then when someone brought Minos his second course and he saw that his beans were TOUCHING his chicken goujons he went

MAD.

And that's when Icarus whispered to his dad that he'd better get the maze right and Daedalus nodded loads.

Then that night before they went to sleep, King Minos came in and took their PILLOWS because he said that he needed them ALL.

And then he counted every single one of his **HEADLESS TEDDIES** and gave them all a kiss goodnight and said that if either of them even **LOOKED** at his teddies there would be **CONSEQUENCES**.

But Icarus couldn't sleep because he said that he **NEEDED** a pillow and that it felt **HORRIBLE** without one and that he wanted to use the **HEADLESS TEDDIES** to make one. But Daedalus said **NO** and that King Minos would probably shave the eyebrows off **BOTH** of them if he found out.

So Icarus shouted, **"FINE!"** And then he just waited until his dad fell asleep and did it anyway.

The next day, Daedalus got to work designing the maze. And he was **DETERMINED** to make it the most difficult maze in the whole of **ANCIENT GREECE**.

So he made sure there were hundreds of CORRIDORS and DEAD ENDS and he even designed a QUADRUPLE LOCK for the room at the very top of the TOWER.

But then when it was the

GRAND OPENING

of the new prison, Daedalus found out that King Minos had put a MINOTAUR inside the maze. And that's when he said that he didn't want anything to do with the maze any more because he knew that MINOTAURS were MONSTERS that looked like HUMAN

BULLS and that they ate HUMAN FLESH and he thought that that was going a bit too far.

So Daedalus told Icarus it was time to go and pack his suitcase and that they were going back to Athens. But Icarus just IGNORED him because he was having a

at the grand opening because there was CANDY FLOSS and a BAND and a giant piñata shaped like a MINOTAUR.

So Daedalus had to pack BOTH of their suitcases. And then he had to stand and wait until the band finished playing their very last song before Icarus would leave.

But then when they went to see King Minos to say goodbye and get Daedalus's money, King Minos said that he wasn't going to pay him and also that he wasn't going to let him LEAVE, either, because he wanted Daedalus to make him loads of other stuff. Like a hairbrush with bristles on BOTH SIDES and slippers with WHEELS on them so he could have comfy feet while he skated around the palace. And a really long stick with a FAKE FINGER on the end that he could use to POKE his servants when they didn't bring his KEBABS fast enough.

But then, Theseus, one of King Minos's prisoners, killed the Minotaur and ESCAPED. And that's when the king said that it must have been DAEDALUS who helped him escape because HE was the only one who knew how the maze WORKED.

And it WAS Daedalus who had helped him because he thought having a MINOTAUR in there was UNFAIR so he gave Theseus's girlfriend, Ariadne, a ball of string for Theseus

and Theseus used it to help him escape the maze. So Daedalus just looked down at his sandals and didn't say anything.

That's when King Minos said that he was FURIOUS because the prison was practically EMPTY and that because of Daedalus he didn't even have a proper number of PRISONERS for it any more.

But then all of a sudden King Minos started brushing his hair REALLY SLOWLY. And then he said, "Or DO I??"

And then he said that he was going to lock DAEDALUS in the tower and that he was going to be his newest PRISONER

FOR LIFE.

But then Icarus said, "That's not FAIR!" because that was Icarus's favourite thing to say and also because he didn't know who was going to give him his POCKET MONEY if his dad wasn't around.

But Minos said that it WAS fair, actually, because he needed a new prisoner for his prison and it was his dad's fault that THESEUS had escaped.

So then Icarus ROLLED HIS EYES and everyone

GASPED

because they all knew that Minos HATED people rolling their eyes because he had a FEAR OF EYEBALLS and he hated seeing them roll about in people's EYE SOCKETS like that.

So that's when Minos yelled, "NOW I HAVE TWO NEW PRISONERS!"

And then he did a REALLY LOUD LAUGH while his guards took Daedalus and Icarus away and even when they were all the way at the top of the tower they could STILL hear Minos laughing below. That's how evil he was.

So Daedalus and Icarus were trapped in

the tower and they didn't even have any games or books so they just had to take turns playing with a bit of wallpaper that had fallen off the wall.

But then one day Daedalus's eyes went WIDE and he said, "I've got a

BRILLIANT PLAN.

I'm going to get us out of here!"

And then he ran over to the window and began COOING at the pigeons.

That's when Icarus started worrying that being trapped in the tower was making his dad go a bit WEIRD (especially when a pigeon landed on the window ledge and Daedalus started SPEAKING to it and asking it for one of its FEATHERS).

So Icarus went over and patted his dad's back and said that he could have TWO TURNS at playing with the piece of

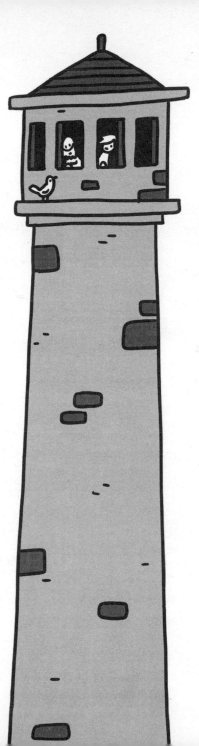

wallpaper if he wanted because he felt sorry for him.

But then the pigeon flew away and left a FEATHER behind and Daedalus GASPED and held it up to Icarus's face and said, "LOOK! This is my PLAN!"

And Icarus said that if his dad's plan was to TICKLE the guards to make them open the door, he wasn't going to be the one doing the tickling.

But Daedalus said they weren't going to be tickling ANYONE. Except maybe THEMSELVES by mistake when they were FLYING with the WINGS he was going to

make for them!

And that's when Icarus GASPED and Daedalus gasped TOO because even though it was his plan he was still a bit SHOCKED at how good it was.

So every day when the guards brought them their lunch, Daedalus said that they should only eat HALF of it and leave the OTHER HALF on the window ledge so that loads of PIGEONS and SEAGULLS would come and leave their FEATHERS behind.

But Icarus didn't listen. And every single day he ate his WHOLE LUNCH and he didn't even leave a TINY CRUMB for the birds because he said that he was STARVING and also that MINI KEBABS were his FAVOURITE.

So it took AGES to get all the feathers that Daedalus needed to make the WINGS and at one point Daedalus told Icarus that if he didn't start sharing his lunch with the birds he would just make ONE pair of wings. And then he gave Icarus a bit of a

LOOK

and Icarus GROANED and threw a tiny bit of kebab on to the window ledge and said,

"Happy now?"

But Daedalus WASN'T happy now because he still needed LOADS of feathers and he knew that it was going to take YEARS if Icarus wasn't going to help.

So that was when he said that if Icarus started sharing his lunch then when they got back to Athens he'd let him have a HOUSE PARTY.

And Icarus's eyes went WIDE and he said, "With pizza?"

And Daedalus said, "Yes."

And Icarus said, "And mini kebabs?"

And Daedalus said, "Yes."

And then Icarus said, "And you'll stay in your bedroom all night and not come out once, even if you need the toilet?"

And Daedalus sighed because it was really hard having a teenager sometimes, especially one like Icarus who wouldn't even give you a bit of his kebab so you could help save his life or let you go to the toilet in your own house.

But Daedalus said yes anyway because he really wanted to get out of the tower.

After a

WHOLE YEAR

Daedalus FINALLY had enough feathers so he waited until Icarus and all the guards were asleep and then he stayed up all night making the wings.

Then Daedalus put on his wings and flapped them in Icarus's face to wake him up. And Icarus was FURIOUS when he woke up but then he saw that his dad had a HUGE grin on his face and also that he was WEARING WINGS.

Icarus leapt out of bed and put his wings on and said he wanted to leave RIGHT AWAY. But Daedalus said that he needed to WAIT and LISTEN TO HIM CLOSELY about the wings and how he had used WAX to stick them together and how that meant they couldn't fly too close to the SUN or the wax would MELT.

And Icarus nodded loads and said, "Uh huh. Uh huh. Let's go!" and then he JUMPED out of the window.

And that just shows you how RIDICULOUS Icarus was because his dad hadn't even told him how to USE the wings yet!

So Daedalus had to jump out after him and yell, "FLAP YOUR WINGS, FOR GOODNESS' SAKE!"

Daedalus was SURE Icarus was going to

land HEAD FIRST on the ground when suddenly a big GUST OF WIND caught Icarus's wings and lifted him up into the air.

That's when Icarus began flapping his wings and flying all over the place. And Daedalus had to shout at him that they were supposed to be ESCAPING but he only listened when one of the guards spotted them and shouted, "GET ME MY SLINGSHOT!"

So that's when Daedalus and Icarus flew away from the palace and away from CRETE and out over the AEGEAN SEA.

But then Icarus started flying a bit HIGH even though his dad had SPECIFICALLY told him not to.

So Daedalus shouted, "Icarus! WHAT did I tell you?!"

And if Icarus was EVER going to listen to his dad then THAT would have been a good time to start. But he didn't. Because he'd spotted a GIRL with LONG HAIR swimming in the water and he wanted to IMPRESS her. (Even though it obviously WASN'T a girl and it was just a bit of seaweed on a rock.) But Icarus didn't know that. And that's probably because he never listened to his dad OR his teachers OR his archery instructor about getting his

EYES TESTED.

So anyway, that's when Icarus started showing off

BIG TIME.

And he kept **WINKING** at the seaweed and flying upside down, and he even did a **TWIRLY THING.**

And then he started to fly HIGHER and HIGHER and Daedalus shouted, "ICARUS! STOP!"

But Icarus didn't listen. He just kept flying higher until his ARMS started to feel a bit WET. And at first Icarus thought it was SWEAT so he tried to wipe it off because he didn't want to get sweat on his toga in front of the girl with the long hair.

But then Icarus GASPED because he realised that it WASN'T sweat and that it was WAX and also that his WINGS WERE MELTING.

And THAT'S when he remembered what

his dad had said about not flying too close to the SUN. But it was too late by then.

And as Icarus fell from the sky he got closer and closer to the SEAWEED ROCK and even though he was FALLING TO HIS DEATH he still shouted, "HEY," at the rock before he hit the water because he wanted to look cool and also because that's how bad his eyesight was.

So that's when I looked at Zach and Zach looked really shocked by the sad ending and I said, "So … do you want to listen to Miss Jones now?"

And Zach said that he did. And also that he

thought he might need glasses. And Maisie said that he should get his eyes tested RIGHT AWAY so that he didn't FALL TO HIS DEATH in the playground and Zach nodded loads.

So that's when he put up his hand and told Miss Jones that he needed to go to the toilet and Miss Jones shut her eyes and took a really deep breath through her nose for ages. And then when she was finished with her breath she opened her eyes and said, "Go. Quickly."

So Zach ran off to the toilet and Miss Jones looked at her watch and ROLLED HER

EYES and Maisie gasped and said, "Miss! You shouldn't roll your eyes. Some people might feed you to a MINOTAUR for doing that!"

Miss Jones looked a bit confused so she must not have known the MYTH. Then when Zack got back she made us walk for AGES until we eventually turned a corner and she yelled, "We're here! We made it!"

And we all looked up and

GASPED

because we were in front of a HUGE

BUILDING and it had STONE PILLARS and LOADS of BIG STEPS and

EVERYTHING.

That's when Jodi nudged me and said that it looked a bit like Ancient Greece and I nodded loads because it DID.

And then all of a sudden a TOUR GUIDE appeared and she said, "Welcome to the BRITISH MUSEUM!"

And before she could even say one more word we asked her if there was a bit about ANCIENT GREECE in the museum and she said that there WAS so we said that we needed her to take us there first and that made her laugh even though we weren't joking.

But then Maisie asked if there would be any MINOTAURS inside and the tour guide said, "Well, you'll just have to wait and find out, won't you?"

And we all GASPED.

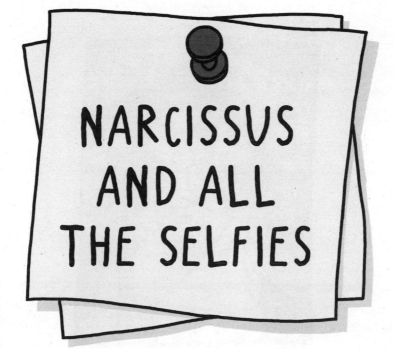

NARCISSUS
AND ALL
THE SELFIES

Characters in
NARCISSUS AND ALL THE SELFIES,
in order of appearance:

NYMPHS, spirits who look after Nature
ECHO, a talkative nymph
HERA, a goddess
NARCISSUS, a vain young man
BABY ZEUS, Narcissus's pet ferret

Izzy has based her version of
the Narcissus myth on the one
told by the Roman poet, Ovid.
Neither the Greek nor the Roman
version feature a ferret in a toga.
Izzy's is the only one to do so,
as far as scholars can tell.

One time when we were at Jodi's house she wouldn't stop taking PHOTOS of herself with her mum's phone even though we were supposed to be playing MONOPOLY and it was her turn.

So that's when me and Jodi got into a bit of an argument because I said that it was RUDE of her to sit and take photos of herself ESPECIALLY when it had been her turn for AGES. But Jodi said that it WASN'T rude so I said that it DEFINITELY WAS and also that she obviously

LOVED HERSELF.

Then Jodi said that she DIDN'T love herself ACTUALLY and that she hadn't even taken that many SELFIES. So that's when I took the phone out of her hand and looked at it and I GASPED because she had taken HUNDREDS OF SELFIES.

And Jodi's face went RED and she said that maybe she HAD got a bit carried away with the photos and that she wouldn't take

any more. And then she asked for the phone back but I said no because I knew that she was just going to take more and that I didn't want her to end up like NARCISSUS.

Jodi got a really confused look on her face when I said that and it was obvious that she didn't know who NARCISSUS was and that I was the only one who knew loads of stuff about MYTHS.

So that's when I explained that in ANCIENT TIMES there used to be all these GODDESSES called NYMPHS who lived in the WOODS and that they were always running around with the DEER and swimming in the LAKES and playing TAG on the mountains.

And usually they all had a great time unless ECHO came along because she was LOUD and a bit ANNOYING and she talked NON-STOP.

Then one day, one of the GREEK GODS called HERA was trying to get a deer to eat an apple out of her hand when Echo appeared and yelled, "HIYA! WHAT ARE YOU DOING? I HURT MY ELBOW. LOOK. IT'S GONE ALL RED. WHAT'S THAT YOU'VE GOT? IS THAT AN APPLE? WHERE DID YOU GET IT?

CAN I HAVE A BIT?"

And the deer ran away.

Hera was RAGING because it had taken her AGES to get the deer to come over to her and feeding a deer an apple from her hand was one of the things she had always wanted to do in life and it was even on her

BUCKET LIST.
1) Feed an apple to a deer
2) Own a pair of
   pure gold sandals
3) Run a marathon
   (when it's been invented)

So that's when Hera said, "I've had ENOUGH of you talking all the time! You are so ANNOYING!"

And Echo said, "No I'm not. YOU ARE!"

And Hera said, "You always have to have the last word, don't you?"

And Echo said, "No, I don't."

So Hera pointed her finger at Echo and said, "Maybe THIS will teach you!" And she used her GODDESS POWERS to put a curse on Echo.

Then Hera said, "My name is Echo and I am SUPER ANNOYING."

And Echo said, "I am

☆– SUPER ANNOYING" –☆

because the CURSE meant that Echo could only say the last thing someone ELSE had just said.

Hera burst out laughing and said, "I eat MUD for my breakfast, I eat MUD for my lunch and I eat MUD for my dinner!"

And Echo said, "I eat MUD for my dinner."

And Hera burst out laughing AGAIN and said that she was going to tell all the other nymphs about THE MUD and also that Echo

was a COPYCAT now.

Echo was FURIOUS with Hera for cursing her and she wanted to tell her to

"GET LOST FOREVER!"

but she couldn't because of the curse.

So Echo went right up to Hera and LICKED HER FACE because she knew that would annoy her because NO ONE likes getting their face licked like that.

Then Hera yelled, "YUCK!

You're DISGUSTING!"

And Echo smiled and said,

"YOU'RE DISGUSTING!"

and then she ran away before Hera could

say anything else.

Echo didn't stop running until she bumped

RIGHT into a boy who was out walking his

pet ferret. And when she looked up at his

face she GASPED because he was PROPER GORGEOUS.

Echo knew RIGHT AWAY that this must be NARCISSUS because he was famous in ANCIENT GREECE for being DROP-DEAD GORGEOUS and all the other nymphs were always talking about him and putting up POSTERS of him in their bedrooms and asking him for his AUTOGRAPH, even

though he always just said, "No. I'm too busy being BEAUTIFUL."

Echo opened her mouth because she wanted to say hi and tell him that her name was Echo and that she liked his bracelets and ask him where he got them and tell him about her sore elbow and ask if he wanted to go swimming.

But when she opened her mouth nothing came out because of the CURSE.

So that's when Narcissus gave her a bit of a WEIRD LOOK and just tried to keep on walking his pet ferret and pretend he hadn't seen her. And it was probably because

Echo was just standing there, opening and shutting her mouth like a fish.

Then all of a sudden Echo started clapping her hands (because she didn't know what else to do and she didn't want the most gorgeous boy she'd ever seen in her life to walk off).

And that's when Narcissus sighed and said, "Look, I'm sort of a BIG DEAL, and I have places to BE. But, are you OK? You look a bit weird."

And Echo said, "You look a bit weird."

And Narcissus GASPED because NO ONE had EVER said to him that he looked

a bit weird before and they had only ever
said that he was

GORGEOUS.

And even though he didn't actually have a
mirror at home, he kept a little bit of paper
in his pocket with the names of everyone
who had told him he was

GORGEOUS

and it had over **NINETY NAMES** on it now
so he knew that he definitely **WAS.**

So that's when Narcissus said, "I'm going away now. My ferret doesn't like you."

And Echo said, "My ferret doesn't like you."

And then all of a sudden Narcissus smiled and said, "Oh! I didn't realise you were out walking your ferret too. I love ferrets!"

And Echo said, "I love ferrets."

And she smiled because she DID love ferrets, actually. Especially the one Narcissus had because it was wearing a mini toga that he had obviously made for it.

Narcissus looked around for ages.

And then he said, "I can't see him. Where's your ferret?"

And Echo sighed because she knew that this was about to get COMPLICATED. And she said, "Where's your ferret?"

That's when Narcissus gave Echo a weird look again and pointed down at his pet ferret and said, "My ferret is right there!"

And Echo said, "My ferret is right there!"

Then Narcissus started to get a bit worried because there DEFINITELY weren't any other ferrets about, just his, which was called Baby Zeus.

So he said, "Wait. Do you think this is YOUR ferret?"

And Echo said, "Do you think this is YOUR ferret?"

And Narcissus

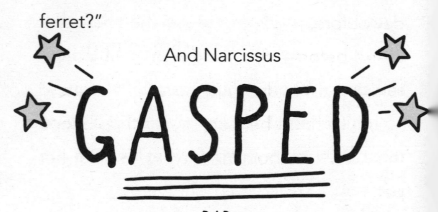

GASPED

and said that he DID think that actually, because Baby Zeus WAS his ferret and he'd had him for YEARS.

But then Echo said that SHE'D had him for years and that's when Narcissus broke down and started CRYING and said that he'd been LYING about having the ferret for years and that he'd actually only just found him the day before.

And before Echo could repeat what he'd said, Narcissus dropped the ferret's lead and ran off because he didn't want her to phone the POLICE about him trying to steal her pet.

And that's when Echo started crying, too. Because she had fallen in LOVE with Narcissus and now he was gone and all she had was a ferret wearing a toga.

So Echo picked up Baby Zeus and went looking for Narcissus. But she couldn't find him anywhere. And that's when she SWORE to the ferret that she would NEVER STOP looking for Narcissus until she found him.

Narcissus ran and hid behind a tree because he was worried that the police were coming to arrest him for being a FERRET STEALER. But then he noticed that he had a bit of MUD on his sandals and he GASPED and forgot all about the police because the sandals were BRAND NEW and he'd wanted them for AGES and they even had these fancy TWIRLY BITS at the back.

So Narcissus went searching for somewhere to wash his sandals and that's when he found a POND surrounded by trees.

Narcissus took his sandals off and bent over to wash them in the pond. And THAT'S when he GASPED because the pond was so STILL that he could see his OWN

REFLECTION in it. And it was the first time that he had ever seen what he looked like and he was so shocked that he shouted, "WOW!

I AM PURE GORGEOUS!"

And that's when everything got a bit WEIRD because Narcissus thought he was SO gorgeous that he actually began to

FANCY HIMSELF a bit.

Narcissus sat there for AGES, looking into the pond and winking at his own reflection and smiling when his reflection winked back. And he forgot all about his muddy sandals and Baby Zeus and he even forgot to go home for his tea.

Then when it got dark and it was time for his bed, Narcissus STILL didn't go home.

He just stayed there, staring at his reflection in the moonlight, because by that point he had

COMPLETELY FALLEN IN LOVE WITH HIMSELF.

Narcissus didn't go home for his tea the next day OR the day after that even though his mum was making chips, cheese and doner kebab, which was his favourite, because he couldn't BEAR not to look at his own reflection for ONE SECOND. So he just stayed in the woods.

And eventually, Narcissus stayed there for so long that he died of hunger and thirst and SUNBURN (because it gets really hot in Greece in July and togas don't have sleeves). And when he died he turned into a long, white flower that leaned over the water so that even when he was dead and had become a flower he could STILL look at his own reflection.

And the whole time Narcissus was sitting there staring at himself in the pond, Echo was wandering around with Baby Zeus looking for him, but she never found him. And it was probably because she was always getting distracted because Baby Zeus's toga belt kept coming undone and she kept having to stop and tie it again.

And even though no one ever saw Echo, or the ferret, ever again, people say that when they are up in the mountains or in the woods or in a cave and they shout something, they can hear Echo repeating their last words. And some people even say they've spotted a GHOST FERRET.

And that's when Zach GASPED and said, "Is that why an echo is called an ECHO?!"

And I nodded because it was.

And that's when Jodi realised how SERIOUS everything was and she SWORE on ALL THE GREEK GODS that she would never ever take even ONE selfie ever again EVER.

And we all said that that was for the best because no one wanted her to die of sunburn.

Then all of a sudden Maisie grabbed Jodi's phone out of my hand and said that she was going to delete EVERY SINGLE PHOTO

Jodi had taken so that Jodi couldn't look at them and fall in love with herself.

But then Jodi said, "WAIT! Can I just keep the good ones?"

And I sighed and shook my head because I knew that I was going to have to tell her the whole Narcissus story

ALL OVER AGAIN!

THE
WOODEN
HORSE TRICK

Characters in
THE WOODEN HORSE TRICK,
in order of appearance:

HELEN, wife of King Menelaus
ZEUS, king of the gods
KING MENELAUS OF SPARTA, Helen's husband
PARIS, Helen's boyfriend
APHRODITE, goddess of love
HERA, goddess of women
ATHENA, goddess of wisdom
KING PRIAM OF TROY, Paris's dad
KING ODYSSEUS OF ITHACA, Greek soldier
and hero
KING AGAMEMNON, Menelaus's brother
ACHILLES, Greek soldier and hero
KING AJAX, Greek soldier and hero
ANTIMACHUS, Trojan soldier
APOLLO, god and son of Zeus

Last week Jodi fell out with Gary Petrie because he took her pencil case out of her drawer in the classroom without even **ASKING** because that's just what he's like. And he used all of Jodi's **GOOD PENS** and he didn't even put the lids back on. And when Jodi saw what Gary Petrie had done, she went

MAD.

Miss Riley said that Jodi needed to **CALM DOWN** and that the lids had only been off for **FIVE MINUTES** and that the pens would probably be FINE. But that's when Jodi got REALLY ANGRY and she shouted that fine wasn't good enough because they had been "PERFECT" before. And then she got sent to the head teacher because we are not allowed to shout at Miss Riley even when we're upset about our pens being

ALMOST RUINED.

Then the next day, Gary Petrie turned up with a GIFT in a BOX for Jodi and he said that he'd made it HIMSELF and that he had done it to say sorry for the PEN THING.

Jodi reached out to take the gift but I shouted, "STOP. It might be a

TRICK!."

and I pulled her arm back before she could touch the box and that's when everyone STARED at me.

So I asked Jodi if she'd ever read the GREEK MYTH about the TROJAN HORSE and she said no. And then all of a sudden there were TWO LOUD GASPS and I turned and saw that our other friends, Zach and Maisie, were STARING at the box in Gary Petrie's hand. And Zach's eyes were SO WIDE they looked like they were going to POP out of his HEAD. And that's when I realised that they DEFINITELY knew about the TROJAN HORSE and how DANGEROUS it was to accept a GIFT from your ENEMY, especially a gift that they had made with their OWN HANDS.

So I did a bit of a FAKE SMILE at Gary Petrie and said, "COULD YOU GIVE US A MINUTE, PLEASE?" because that's what my mum says to people when she needs them to go away so that she can have a WORD with me and sometimes with Dad.

And that's when I started telling Jodi that, ages and ages ago, in Ancient Greece, there was this woman called Helen.

Some people think she was born from an egg (which is a bit weird) and her dad was actually a GREEK GOD called ZEUS, which meant that she was really popular at school because her dad was famous, but it was also really annoying for her because sometimes he would shout things at her from the clouds like, "I can SEE what you're DOING, Helen!" and "Me and your mum already told you, you're only allowed ONE sweet at breaktime!" and "WASH YOUR HANDS FOR THE LOVE OF ZEUS!"

So anyway, when Helen grew up she married this man called KING MENELAUS OF SPARTA (but everyone just called him Menelaus and sometimes M-Dog because it took too long to say the whole thing all the time).

Helen was really pretty and she was good at

loads of stuff like PAINTING and SINGING and YODELLING and King Menelaus thought she was the

BEST THING EVER.

But then he got a bit WEIRD and CLINGY and he kept telling Helen that he wanted her to stand RIGHT NEXT TO HIM all the time and that really got on her NERVES because she wanted to stand wherever she LIKED and she didn't need him telling her where she could STAND.

Then one day, Paris, a young prince from

a place called TROY, visited the palace. He'd heard their CARPETS were the FLUFFIEST carpets EVER and he wanted to feel them for himself before he asked his mum and dad for one for his bedroom. He was also visiting because of something that happened at a wedding he went to.

At the wedding, instead of throwing a bouquet of FLOWERS like normal people do, someone had thrown a GOLDEN APPLE with the words "FOR THE MOST GORGEOUS" on it. And ALL the gods started fighting over it because they wanted to be the MOST GORGEOUS.

ZEUS almost got it until APHRODITE put him in a HEADLOCK and grabbed it off him. And that's when things got OUT OF HAND because HERA started screaming that the apple was OBVIOUSLY HERS and then ATHENA said that if SOMEONE didn't

put the golden apple in her hand RIGHT NOW she was going to start an ACTUAL WAR.

So eventually someone said that PARIS should decide who deserved the GOLDEN APPLE and Hera said that if he picked her then she would make him the most powerful man on EARTH. And Athena said that if he picked HER then she would make sure that he won any FIGHTS that he got into. But Paris said that what they were doing was WRONG because fighting over who was MOST GORGEOUS was SILLY and that he wasn't going to judge them

on their LOOKS.

But then Aphrodite said that if he picked HER, she would make sure that the MOST GORGEOUS woman in the world fell in love with him, and that woman was Helen of Sparta. And that's when Paris changed his mind and picked Aphrodite.

When Helen first saw Paris, he had his back to her because he was doing up his sandal. She thought he was a GIRL because he was called PARIS and because he was wearing the same hairband as her. But when he stood up she saw that he was a man and also that he was STARING at her and smiling LOADS.

But Helen didn't mind Paris staring and smiling at her. And she was actually staring at HIM a bit too, because he had a really nice PERM in his hair, which his dad had done for him.

Helen and Paris went for a walk together because Paris had forgotten to bring a bobble for his hair and Helen said that she had loads of spare ones and he said that he'd go with her to get it. And Helen even took Paris the LONG WAY because she wanted to spend more time speaking to him and that's when they found out that they had LOADS in common because they both collected BELTS and SHOES and they even used the same HAIR CONDITIONER.

Then Paris said that he had to go home because his mum was making his tea but that she could come too if she wanted and that she could live with him in his parents' palace in Troy. Helen really liked Paris because he was NICE and KIND and he didn't tell her where to stand all the time. And then Paris said that he

♡ LOVED HER ALREADY ♡

and also that she could have his BELT

COLLECTION and her own TRIPLE WARDROBE for all her TUNICS and that his dad, King Priam, would even give her a PERM if she wanted.

So Helen said no to the perm but yes to moving to Troy with Paris, so they sneaked off together. And they took LOADS of stuff with them, like all the GOLD VASES and SILVER CUTLERY and King Menelaus's new CAPPUCCINO MACHINE.

And Paris had even tried to take a bit of the CARPET but Helen said that that was going TOO FAR so he didn't.

When King Menelaus found out, he was

RAGING

and he kept shouting that Helen was **HIS** and that he was a **KING** and that Paris was only a **PRINCE** and that **HIS** sandals were **MUCH** nicer than the ones Paris had been wearing.

King Menelaus said that he was going to go to Troy and get Helen **BACK**. Then he asked all his **KING PALS** if they would come with him for **BACKUP** because he didn't know if Paris had any big brothers or anything like that. And they all said yes and that they'd

bring their ARMIES too because they thought it was really cheeky of Paris to come to Ancient Greece and steal Menelaus's wife and also because they knew that King Menelaus would just keep asking them, over and over, until they said yes because that was just what he was like.

But then KING ODYSSEUS OF ITHACA said that he couldn't go to Troy because he'd forgotten that he was supposed to be getting his hair cut the next day.

So that's when everyone started saying, "OH COME ON, ODDY!" because they all called him Oddy and also because they knew that he was probably just LYING about his HAIR APPOINTMENT and that he just wanted to stay at home all day eating grapes.

But Odysseus said that he WASN'T lying and that it had taken him MONTHS to get the appointment and that it was with the best hairdresser in the whole of ANCIENT GREECE. So that's when King Agamemnon leaned over and whispered to Odysseus that if he didn't come then he'd tell EVERYONE about him not being able to tie his own SANDALS and Odysseus's face went a bit red and he said that he would go.

So all the kings started getting their ARMIES together and Odysseus went looking for ACHILLES because he was the BEST WARRIOR in all of Ancient Greece.

Then the next day, King Menelaus and all his king pals packed loads of SANDWICHES and JUICE and PUZZLES and got in their boats and began to sail across the Aegean

Sea to Troy. Menelaus said that he was going to pick one of his king pals to be in charge of the MISSION because he needed to finish a POEM and also a SOCK BUNNY that he was making for Helen. And then he said that he wouldn't be doing any of the ROWING either because he needed to save his

ARM STRENGTH

for fighting Paris

TO THE DEATH.

ALL the kings wanted to be in CHARGE because then they would get to order EVERYONE about and make the first SANDCASTLE when they reached the beach at Troy.

But Menelaus chose Agamemnon and everyone TUTTED and rolled their EYES because they all knew that Menelaus had picked Agamemnon because they were BROTHERS.

But Menelaus said that that was RUBBISH and that he'd picked Agamemnon because he'd brought the most SHIPS. And when Menelaus said that he gave another of the kings, KING AJAX, a bit of a LOOK because Agamemnon had brought ONE HUNDRED ships and Ajax had only brought TWELVE. And Ajax didn't do any more tutting after that.

Having Agamemnon in charge was a

NIGHTMARE

because he LOVED IT and he kept making everyone do loads of stuff for him like cut the CRUSTS off his cheese sandwiches and polish every single bit of the ONE-THOUSAND-PIECE JIGSAW that he'd brought with him for when he was bored of rowing.

But when they got to Troy, Agamemnon got a **WEIRD LOOK** on his face and it was **OBVIOUS** that he wished he wasn't in charge any more and it was probably because the city of Troy was completely surrounded by huge **STONE WALLS** guarded by **TROJAN SOLDIERS** who had **SPEARS** and **SPIKES** and **REALLY MEAN LOOKS** on their faces.

So Agamemnon asked if anyone **ELSE** would like a turn at being **COMMANDER-IN-CHIEF** but everyone just shook their heads and looked down at their sandals. Then Odysseus said that he thought they should knock on the GATES OF TROY and ask for Helen. And Menelaus nodded LOADS and said that he would go too and also that they should ask about his CAPPUCCINO MACHINE.

So Odysseus and

Menelaus went up to the gates and knocked for ages but no one answered. Then a TROJAN MAN called ANTIMACHUS stuck his head out of a little hole in the door and shouted, "You lot are NEVER getting in here. So you can CLEAR OFF!"

Odysseus was RAGING after that because he'd just been trying to sort everything out

NICELY. And Menelaus was annoyed TOO because he was SURE that he'd smelled CAPPUCCINO on Antimachus's breath.

So that's when Agamemnon said that it was

WAR

and then he told everyone to start climbing the walls. So they did. But they kept slipping down because of their sandals. Especially Achilles because he'd always had a bit of a dodgy ankle. And even when they DID reach the top, the Trojan guards would just stamp on their fingers until they fell back again.

But Agamemnon kept making them try, again and again, until eventually Achilles started CRYING and saying that he wanted to go home because he'd already had his fingers stamped on TWICE and also because the straps on his sandals had snapped.

But Agamemnon said NO and that they weren't leaving without HELEN.

And then all of a sudden Achilles stopped complaining about his sandals and it wasn't because he'd managed to fix them or because all the other soldiers were rolling their eyes at him, it was because someone

had shot him right in his dodgy ankle with an ARROW and he was dead.

Now Agamemnon was RAGING about Achilles being dead and he shouted, "WHO DID THAT?!" over the wall and a voice said, "IT WAS ME! PARIS! And the god APOLLO helped me so you'd all better GET LOST or you'll get the SAME!"

So that's when Agamemnon said, "THIS IS WAR!" and everyone nodded because

they already knew that it was war. But then Agamemnon said, "No. I mean, this is REALLY war now. LET'S GET THEM!" And all the Greek soldiers CHEERED.

Then Agamemnon took something out from underneath his TOGA and smiled. And then he shouted, "PARIS? ARE YOU STILL THERE?"

And Paris said, "NO!"

And Agamemnon said, "I'VE FOUND SOMETHING OVER HERE. IT LOOKS LIKE A CAN OF HAIRSPRAY."

And Paris GASPED and shouted, "THAT'S MINE! THROW IT OVER!" because he hadn't been able to get out to the shops to buy hairspray and his PERM was a bit of a state.

So Agamemnon winked at the other Greek soldiers and then SHOOK the can loads and threw it over the wall.

And as SOON as it landed Paris started spraying it ALL OVER his hair until he realised that it didn't SMELL like hairspray and that it looked a bit GREEN and that he couldn't really BREATHE any more.

Then Agamemnon shouted, "PARIS? ARE YOU STILL THERE?"

But Paris didn't say anything this time and

Agamemnon knew that that meant he was **DEAD** because the hairspray wasn't hairspray because it was actually **POISON**.

Then Agamemnon said that they should all sit on each other's **SHOULDERS** and fight the **TROJAN-WALL GUARDS** that way but that only lasted about five minutes before there weren't enough Greeks left because they all had ARROWS through their ARMS and LEGS and HEADS.

So the kings went and got even MORE soldiers and soon there were THOUSANDS of Ancient Greeks trying to get over the walls.

But nothing worked. The Greek army couldn't get in and all the Trojan people were trapped inside. And it wouldn't have mattered HOW many sandwiches King Menelaus had brought, they STILL would have run out because believe it or not they stayed there for TEN WHOLE YEARS trying to climb the walls.

EVERYONE had had enough and they kept asking Agamemnon if they could just go home now because it was OBVIOUS that they were never going to get past the walls and loads of them had WAR WOUNDS and none of them had any clean pants left.

But Agamemnon said that it was up to Menelaus because Helen was HIS wife. And that's when Menelaus said that he didn't care if it took ANOTHER TEN YEARS, he wasn't going ANYWHERE without Helen. And they probably should have just given up and gone home because if you knock on someone's door for ten years and they don't answer even though they're home then it's pretty OBVIOUS that they don't want to see you and that you should just take the hint.

But that just shows you how STUBBORN and SELFISH Menelaus was because he was only thinking about HIMSELF and what HE wanted and he definitely wasn't thinking about what HELEN wanted OR what all his KING PALS wanted OR about all the TROJAN PEOPLE trapped inside the walls that couldn't get out to go to the SHOPS because of the Greek soldiers laying SEIGE to the city.

Then one day Odysseus said that he had an IDEA. And then he started drawing loads of pictures of HORSES and saying that he wanted to make the BIGGEST wooden horse in the WORLD. But everyone just ignored him because they didn't see how making a wooden horse was going to help anything and also because they thought that he was just doing it to get ATTENTION.

So that's when Odysseus said that he had a

SECRET PLAN

to do with the HORSE and then he whispered something to Agamemnon and Menelaus. And Menelaus's eyes went WIDE and he shouted, "CUT DOWN ALL THE TREES TO MAKE THE HORSE. NOW!"

But then Agamemnon did that thing when you clear your throat and make a noise to get everyone's attention and everyone knew he was doing it to REMIND Menelaus that he wasn't the one in charge and that he shouldn't be giving ORDERS.

So Menelaus said sorry and Agamemnon said that it was OK.

And then Agamemnon shouted, "CUT

DOWN ALL THE TREES TO MAKE THE HORSE. NOW!"

So everyone started chopping down trees and building the giant horse. And it only took them ONE WEEK to do it because the ANCIENT GREEKS were really good at MAKING STUFF and they are actually the ones who INVENTED loads of stuff that we have today like LIGHTHOUSES and the OLYMPIC GAMES and even ALARM CLOCKS.

Odysseus went around whispering in everyone's ears about the SECRET PLAN and every single person GASPED when they

heard it because it was a

BRILLIANT PLAN

and also because they were shocked at how SNEAKY it was.

As soon as it got dark, Agamemnon and the rest of the Greeks wheeled the horse up to the gates of Troy and opened a SECRET DOOR in the horse's STOMACH and Odysseus and some of the BEST soldiers climbed inside.

Then Menelaus stuck a note on the horse that said he was sorry for climbing the walls

and trying to steal
his wife back for ten
years and that the
giant horse was a
LEAVING GIFT.

And then they all made a BIG SHOW of packing up their SPEARS and TENTS and all their JIGSAWS and Menelaus kept shouting, "OH, WELL. WE'D BETTER GET HOME TO GREECE THEN. TIME TO GO."

Then Menelaus and the rest of the Greeks got in their boats. But they DIDN'T go home. They just sailed around the corner and waited. Because the horse obviously WASN'T a leaving gift and the Greeks were only PRETENDING to give up.

It took the Trojans AGES to do anything about the giant wooden horse because

EVERY SINGLE MEMBER OF THE TROJAN ARMY said that King Priam should just leave it OUTSIDE because they didn't know what was going on.

But as SOON as King Priam saw the horse he shouted, "That horse is PURE GORGEOUS. Open the gates!"

And then he ran out and started stroking the wooden horse all over its body because he LOVED horses and he'd never DREAMED that he would be lucky enough to own a giant wooden one.

The soldiers hiding inside the horse had to stay COMPLETELY SILENT because they didn't want anyone to know they were in there. But that was really hard because King Priam kept **WHISPERING** to the horse that he

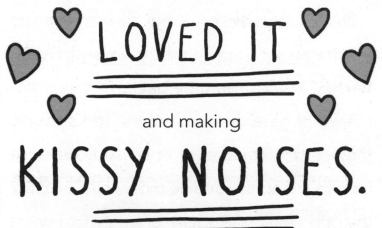

LOVED IT

and making

KISSY NOISES.

And all the soldiers had to put their hands over their mouths and bite the inside of their cheeks to stop themselves from laughing.

Then Priam found Menelaus's note and he SQUEALED with happiness and told everyone that the Greeks were GONE FOR GOOD and EVERYONE cheered.

The Greek soldiers held their breath as the Trojan army wheeled the horse through the gates and into Troy because they were scared of getting caught and also because Odysseus had eaten a WEIRD FISH that he'd found on the beach and he had a SORE TUMMY.

The Greeks stayed inside the horse while the Trojans had a huge BARBECUE PARTY because FINALLY someone had been able to get out to go to the BIG SUPERMARKET and they hadn't had any BURGERS for AGES.

The Trojans went WILD that night because they thought THE WAR between them and the Ancient Greeks was FINALLY OVER and that everyone could relax now and get a good sleep without having to listen to Menelaus shouting "COME HOME, BABY CAKES" over the walls to Helen in the middle of the night.

Odysseus and the Greek soldiers waited PATIENTLY inside the horse while everyone had the party around them. And it

wasn't easy because it was REALLY HOT inside the horse and they were STARVING because Agamemnon had forgotten to give them a packed lunch and they could SMELL the burgers.

As soon as the Trojans EVENTUALLY stopped partying and went to bed King Menelaus and the rest of the Ancient Greeks sailed their ships back around the corner and sneaked ashore on their TIPTOES and waited outside the gates.

Then Odysseus and his soldiers climbed out of the horse's stomach and ate all the barbecue LEFTOVERS. And they

were SO HUNGRY that they completely forgot that they were supposed to be on a DANGEROUS MISSION and also that there were THOUSANDS OF GREEK SOLDIERS waiting to be let in.

But then all of a sudden they heard a voice say, "PSSSST!" and they all gasped and dropped their food on the ground and ran over and OPENED THE GATES TO TROY.

Odysseus and the soldiers stood up really straight and tried to pretend like they hadn't been eating the leftovers even though it was OBVIOUS because they had KETCHUP all

over their faces and Odysseus had even dribbled some down his TUNIC.

Agamemnon gave Odysseus a LOOK but Menelaus didn't even NOTICE the ketchup because he was too busy storming around Troy crying, "BABY CAKES! BABY CAKES!"

That's when Priam appeared in his HORSEY PYJAMAS and when he saw MENELAUS and the GREEK ARMY and the HOLE in the wooden horse's stomach he started SCREAMING for the TROJAN ARMY. But the Trojan army were FAST ASLEEP because they were EXHAUSTED from eating all the BURGERS and HOTDOGS and CHICKEN-ON-A-STICK.

And that's when Priam started CRYING and saying Helen didn't even LIVE with them any more and that she lived in her OWN HOUSE at the other side of Troy and that's when King Menelaus found out that he'd been shouting over the WRONG WALL for ten years.

King Menelaus told Priam EXACTLY

what he thought of his son taking his BABY CAKES and Priam just stood there listening and didn't say anything back. And then when Menelaus eventually stopped shouting, Priam said, "Are you finished?" And Menelaus said that he was, actually. And so Priam said that he needed to ask him something and that now probably wasn't the right time but that if he didn't ask him now then he might NEVER get a chance to ask him because they were probably about to

FIGHT TO THE DEATH.

So Menelaus said OK. And that's when Priam said that he needed to know where he'd got his CARPETS from and that it had been his son's DYING WISH to know because he'd tried to get the same one for his bedroom but he said it wasn't NEARLY as soft as the one in King Menelaus's palace and it had been bothering him for TEN YEARS.

But Menelaus just LAUGHED and said there was NO WAY he was telling him because his son had stolen his WIFE and he wasn't going to let him COPY HIS CARPETS!

Menelaus was just about to DRAW HIS SWORD and chop Priam's permy head off when HELEN appeared. And even though he hadn't seen her for ten years he recognised her RIGHT AWAY even though she had a shaved head now.

King Menelaus was just about to ask what happened to her head when Helen held up her hand and said, "BEFORE you ask, SOMEONE tried to give me a PERM."

And that's when Helen looked at Priam and Priam looked down at the ground and Menelaus knew RIGHT AWAY that that must be the reason that Helen had moved

out of Paris's mum and dad's house.

But then one of the TROJAN SOLDIERS appeared because he needed to use the water fountain because he was THIRSTY from eating all the MEAT. And when he saw King Menelaus and THOUSANDS of ANCIENT GREEKS he ran off to wake up the rest of the Trojan army.

So Menelaus told one of his soldiers to take Helen to the boat and then the Greeks and the Trojans had an EPIC BATTLE. And there were SWORDS and HEADS and BURGERS flying around EVERYWHERE. And the gods watched the WHOLE THING and Zeus even made them all POPCORN because the gods were a bit sick like that and they enjoyed watching wars and arguments and people falling off their horses. And at one point they even got involved and did stuff like untie people's SANDALS and then laugh when they fell over.

Aphrodite was LOVING watching all the trouble she'd caused but Athena said that she was getting a bit BORED so she decided to make the giant wooden horse WOBBLE and Odysseus shouted, "RUN!"

So all the Greeks ran out of Troy and sailed back to ANCIENT GREECE.

Helen started shouting at Menelaus THE SECOND he got on the boat because she was RAGING about how he thought he could just TAKE her back to Sparta without even ASKING if that's what she wanted.

So that's when King Menelaus said sorry and asked if there was anything he could do to make it better. And she said yes and that he could make sure that he didn't stand so close to her when they got home and that she needed more SPACE especially because she needed to keep practising her YODELLING now that she was a PROFESSIONAL YODELLER.

And then Helen smiled and asked him if he wanted to hear and that she'd been practising for ten years and Menelaus said yes.

Then when Helen was finished King Menelaus looked a bit worried and he asked her if she was going to YODEL at him again because he didn't like it and he was starting to think that maybe it had been a bit of a bad idea to go to Troy and get her after all.

And Helen said that she WAS and that she was going to yodel ALL THE WAY BACK TO ANCIENT GREECE. And that's when everyone GROANED because they all knew

that it was going to be a LONG JOURNEY.

So then I asked Jodi if she still wanted to accept the gift that Gary Petrie had made for her and she said no.

But then after lunch she said that she'd CHANGED HER MIND and that she wanted the gift and that she couldn't stop THINKING about it and that just because stuff like that happened in ANCIENT GREECE it didn't mean that it was going to happen at OUR SCHOOL.

So I didn't say anything else to try to stop her because there's not much you can do once Jodi has made up her mind about something and also because I wanted to see what was inside the box.

So we went up to Gary and Gary handed Jodi

THE BOX.

And even though I couldn't see inside I knew RIGHT AWAY that it was something BAD because Jodi's face went RED and her eye started TWITCHING a bit.

Then Gary started LAUGHING and saying, "What? I thought you'd LOVE IT!"

And I looked and saw that it was a

HOMEMADE BADGE and that it said

on it.

And that's when Jodi took an apple out of her bag and wrote **"THE MOST ANNOYING OF ALL"** on it and threw it **RIGHT** at Gary Petrie!

KING MIDAS'S
MEGA-BAD
DECISIONS

Characters in
KING MIDAS'S MEGA-BAD DECISIONS,
in order of appearance:

KING MIDAS, a foolish man
SILENUS the SATYR, a woodland god
DIONYSUS, god of fun
THE QUEEN, King Midas's wife
PAN, god of the outdoors
ZEUS, king of the gods
APOLLO, the most beautiful god of all
ANTONIO, King Midas's hairdresser

One time when it was our school TALENT SHOW the head teacher, Mr Graves, said that there should be a PUPIL JUDGE on the judging panel.

We all thought that was a REALLY good idea because usually it is just teachers and office ladies and one time the lollipop man who are the judges, and they are all quite old so they don't really know about YOUNG STUFF which means they sometimes choose the wrong winner.

That's when Mr Graves said that annoying GARY PETRIE could be a judge because he was the one who'd found the class

HAMSTER under the RECYCLING BINS last week.

So we started doing our talents but AS SOON as Mika had had his go, Gary stood up and started clapping LOADS. And then he said that he didn't even NEED to see any more because he thought Mika should definitely win.

I was FURIOUS when Gary said that. And so was Jodi. And she even shouted, "Are you being ACTUALLY SERIOUS?!" Because mine and Jodi's dance routine was OBVIOUSLY the best because we'd even jumped off the stage into the AUDIENCE during our performance and Jodi had tried to do the SPLITS at the end and EVERYTHING.

EVERYONE knew that the only reason Gary picked Mika to be the winner was because they were BEST FRIENDS. What

Mika had done wasn't even a talent because all he'd done was put his hood up and wave one hand about to some music and say that he was a RAPPER (even though he didn't actually do any rapping or say even one word!).

So that's when I said that I needed to have

with the judges because it is NOT OK to make someone be the WINNER just because they are your BEST FRIEND. You should make someone the winner because their dance is obviously the best!

So I went up to the judges' table and said all of that. And Jodi came too and she stood with her hands on her hips and gave Gary Petrie a

LOOK.

And that's when I told the judges that Gary needed to be SACKED

because he was being just like KING MIDAS from ANCIENT GREEK TIMES and Jodi said, "YEAH!" even though I was pretty sure she didn't know who King Midas was.

But Gary said that if he was like a KING then that meant he should DEFINITELY get to pick the winner because kings are better then TEACHERS.

So that's when I put both my hands down on the judging table and looked RIGHT into Gary's eyes and said, "How would you feel if you got DONKEY EARS?!"

Gary didn't say anything back. But I could tell by the look on his face that he wouldn't

"

like it and also that he had no idea what I was talking about.

So that's when I explained that there used to be this king called **KING MIDAS** and how one time his servants brought him this man who was wandering around the palace gardens, picking all the fruit from the palace trees and eating it without even asking or **WASHING** it first.

But when King Midas saw the man he got quite a **SHOCK** because the man wasn't even a **MAN** because he was a **SATYR** which is a half-man half-horse person.

King Midas leaned forward on his throne

and looked a bit closer at the SATYR and that's when he saw that he was wearing a T-shirt that said **"ROCK GODS"** and he knew that that was the name of the band that the Greek God DIONYSUS was in.

So he asked the satyr what his name was and if he

knew Dionysus and the satyr said that his name was SILENUS and that he played in the same BAND as Dionysus. And that the band was on TOUR in Ancient Greece and that he'd gone to get something for his breakfast that morning but got lost and that he was starving because it was past lunchtime now.

So King Midas made Silenus a cheese-and-ham sandwich because he knew that you needed to treat friends of the GREEK GODS very well and do stuff like make them sandwiches when they were starving so that the Greek gods didn't get annoyed and put a CURSE on you. And he even cut the sandwich into little triangles and put some FANCY CRISPS on the side of the plate.

As soon as Silenus had finished his sandwich, King Midas gave him a ride to where the band were playing on his horse and he knew exactly where to go because there were posters about the show EVERYWHERE because the

ROCK GODS

were probably the most popular band in all

of Ancient Greece.

When they arrived, Silenus took King Midas BACKSTAGE, which Midas thought was BRILLIANT because he'd never been to a ROCK CONCERT before and he'd definitely never been backstage.

As soon as the god Dionysus saw Silenus he cheered and gave him a big hug and then he shook King Midas's hand for ages because he'd been really worried about how they were going to do their gig without their triangle player.

Dionysus was SO grateful, he told King Midas that he was going to grant him

ONE WISH and that the wish could be ANYTHING he wanted.

EVERYONE thought that King Midas was going to ask for TEN HORSES or a MILLION POUNDS or even a SIGNED ROCK GODS T-SHIRT. But he didn't.

Midas said that he wanted EVERYTHING that he touched to turn to gold.

And that's when Dionysus and the other band members all looked at each other and Dionysus said, "Are you SURE??"

And King Midas nodded and said that he DEFINITELY WAS because King Midas was MEGA-GREEDY and also he wasn't

very smart.

So Dionysus granted Midas his wish and then the band went on stage.

King Midas was SO EXCITED about the GOLD THING that he ran out of the concert hall and LEAPT on to his horse because he couldn't wait to get home and tell his wife that he could MAKE GOLD.

But King Midas didn't get very far because his BUM turned the horse to SOLID GOLD.

At first, King Midas was upset because he quite liked his horse. But then he realised that he had a SOLID GOLD HORSE now and he decided that he wasn't that upset any more because GOLD!

It took King Midas AGES to get home because everything he touched kept turning to GOLD, like little STONES that got inside his sandals and a TWIG that he picked from a tree and a PARK BENCH that he sat on when he needed a rest.

And by the time he got home he was starting to wonder if maybe he had made a mistake asking for the

GOLD POWERS

because his back was really sore from carrying the bench and the horse, and when he tried to put his slippers on they turned to gold. And even though gold slippers look nice and shiny, they're not very comfortable.

Then when King Midas was trying to eat his tea, all his food kept turning to gold as SOON as it touched his mouth. And by the end of the meal King Midas had a plate FULL of little gold peas and SOLID GOLD FISH FINGERS and his stomach was rumbling like MAD.

So that's when King Midas told his wife that he was going back to see the BAND to ask if Dionysus would let him EXCHANGE his wish.

And that's when his wife got a bit of a weird look on her face and he just KNEW that it was because she LOVED GOLD and that it didn't matter how many gold NECKLACES and RINGS and TEDDIES she had she always wanted MORE.

So King Midas sighed and said, "Fine. What do you want me to touch before I go?"

And the queen said that it was a bit

EMBARRASSING

but that she had ALWAYS wanted a SOLID GOLD TOILET SEAT. So King Midas sighed and went upstairs and sat on the toilet seat until it turned to gold and that made the queen really happy.

Then when Midas EVENTUALLY arrived at the ROCK GODS concert he managed to catch Dionysus just as he was about to get on the TOUR BUS and ask him about the EXCHANGING-HIS-WISH THING.

Dionysus rolled his eyes and said that the GREEK GODS didn't do exchanges OR refunds but that he WOULD help him get rid of the GOLD THING.

So Dionysus told King Midas to go to the river Pactolus and have a swim in it and that that would take away his

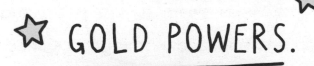

GOLD POWERS.

And then he looked Midas RIGHT in the eyes and said that he needed to stop being so GREEDY and start making BETTER CHOICES.

And King Midas nodded loads and said he would and then he RAN all the way to the river and jumped in with his clothes on and he didn't even take his sandals off first.

Then all of a sudden the water turned GLITTERY and SHIMMERY and King Midas just KNEW that it was the gold coming out of him.

So King Midas swam to the shore and touched a stone and nothing happened.

And then he touched the foot of a god called Pan who was walking past and THAT didn't turn to gold either.

So Midas shouted, "I'M FREE OF MY GOLD!"

And that's when Gary interrupted me and said that he didn't think King Midas having a GOLD TOILET SEAT had anything to do with him and that I hadn't even mentioned any DONKEY EARS.

So that's when I said that it had EVERYTHING to do with him and that I was JUST about to get to the DONKEY EARS bit if he could just be patient for ONCE in his entire life.

And then I explained that King Midas never learned ANYTHING from the whole GOLD THING and that he kept ON making bad choices until one of the Greek gods EVENTUALLY put a curse on him.

Then Gary went quiet and sat down again and I knew that it was because he was a bit worried about

CURSES.

So I explained that King Midas and the god Pan ended up becoming pals and that one day Pan asked Midas if he would be a judge for a talent show the GREEK GODS were having because they LOVED doing talent shows and they were always showing off and saying that they were better than each other, especially Zeus.

So anyway, all the Greek gods got up on stage and did loads of stuff like SINGING and WEIGHT LIFTING and WALKING LIKE A CRAB. And at the end of the talent show it was only PAN and APOLLO who were left and they were each meant to do a FINAL PERFORMANCE and then King Midas had to choose the winner.

But then before Apollo could even tune his guitar properly, King Midas said that he didn't even need to HEAR him play because PAN was obviously the winner. And then King Midas jumped up and shook Pan's hand and loads of confetti and balloons fell from the ceiling and the crowd cheered.

But Apollo was FURIOUS because he knew that HE should have won because he was at least

ONE MILLION
TIMES
BETTER

than Pan because he could play the electric guitar REALLY FAST and Pan could only play the recorder. And Apollo knew that King Midas and Pan were BEST FRIENDS and that that was obviously the reason King Midas had made him the winner.

So that's when Apollo looked RIGHT at King Midas and yelled, "If you think Pan's better than ME then your ears are obviously TOO SMALL TO HEAR WITH!"

Everyone

and looked at King Midas's ears when Apollo said that. And, to be fair, even though King Midas got a bit upset and kept saying that he had PERFECTLY NORMAL-SIZED

EARS loads of people agreed that they probably WERE a bit too small.

And then Apollo pointed his guitar at Midas and a CURSE came out of it and hit Midas RIGHT on the ears and turned his tiny king ears into long, floppy DONKEY'S EARS.

King Midas covered his ears with his hands and ran offstage and locked himself in the dressing room before anyone could see them.

And he got the shock of his LIFE when he looked into the mirror and saw his new ears because they were MASSIVE and GREY

and HAIRY and the only thing King Midas
actually liked about them was that they were
so big that they made his nose look a bit
smaller.

But then all of a sudden someone knocked on the changing-room door and King Midas started to

PANIC

because he knew that if people knew about his ears that they would LAUGH at him and call him names like "BIG EARS" or "LONG LOBES" or "JIMMY JUG LUGS".

So he ran to the costume cupboard and pulled out a SCARF and wrapped it around his giant ears and head like a TURBAN and it was actually his WIFE at the door and she said that she liked the king's new TURBAN and that she liked it so much she thought he should wear it ALL THE TIME.

King Midas was REALLY happy when the queen said that because he was worried that if she ever saw his ears that she wouldn't like him any more because she was really scared of HORSES and he knew that donkeys are basically just small horses.

So King Midas wore his turban every day and he even wore one to bed and no one in the whole of ANCIENT GREECE knew about his donkey ears.

But then one day King Midas was trying to make cereal for his breakfast and he poured SO much milk in the bowl that it went ALL OVER the table and the queen told him

off a bit and said that he needed to get his
FRINGE cut because it kept falling out of
his turban and he obviously couldn't see.

So King Midas phoned his hairdresser and
managed to get an

EMERGENCY APPOINTMENT

after he told him about the CEREAL THING.

But then when he got there he realised
that he was going to have to take his turban
OFF and that his hairdresser was going to
see his DONKEY EARS.

So that's when King Midas asked his

hairdresser if he could keep a

SECRET.

And his hairdresser put down his scissors and said, "I, ANTONIO" (because that was his name) "SWEAR ON ALL THE GREEK GODS THAT I WILL NEVER EVER TELL ANYONE YOUR SECRET EVER!"

And that made King Midas happy so he sat down and took a sip of his cappuccino and started to unwrap his turban.

But then as SOON as one of his big donkey ears flopped out Antonio GASPED and covered his mouth with both of his hands.

So King Midas reminded Antonio about how he had sworn on **ALL THE GREEK GODS** and Antonio nodded loads and started to cut King Midas's fringe and tried not to think about the **MASSIVE DONKEY EARS.**

But then as soon as the king left, Antonio RAN out of the shop and all the way to the nearest field and dug a huge hole and then shouted the secret into it and then filled the hole back up with mud. And even though it made no sense at ALL to do that, it made Antonio feel a bit better because even though he had told King Midas that he was good at keeping secrets he really WASN'T and he didn't want the GREEK GODS putting a CURSE on him too.

But as SOON as Antonio went off for his four o'clock appointment these really weird PLANTS started to grow out from the place

where he had whispered the secret and then every time the WIND rustled them it sort of gave them the power to SPEAK (which is a bit creepy).

And the plants said, "King Midas has donkey's ears! King Midas has donkey's ears!"

And because the hole that Antonio had whispered the secret into was actually right next to the best KEBAB SHOP in all of ANCIENT GREECE, it wasn't long before everyone knew King Midas's hairy secret.

So that's when I stood up straight and crossed my arms and looked at Gary Petrie

and said, "Well?"

And he said, "Well what?"

And I said, "Do you think it's maybe time to stop making

BAD

decisions, Gary? I think you've made **ENOUGH** of those this week, haven't you??"

And Gary Petrie got a bit of a weird look on his face.

And I knew that he knew that I knew that

HE was the one who had left the class hamster's cage open and that it was HIS fault that Susan got out and that he should have told the truth instead of smiling and getting his photo taken with a certificate that Mr Killington had made for him that said he was a HERO.

GARY IS A HERO. ☑

And that's when Gary said that he was feeling a bit UNWELL all of a sudden and that maybe someone else should do the judging.

I smiled and said that that sounded like a

VERY GOOD IDEA

because it did and also because I knew that that meant that we might still win. Then Gary asked Miss Jones if he could borrow the little mirror we know that she keeps in her bag that she uses to put her lipstick back on after lunch.

So Miss Jones asked him why he needed a mirror and Gary's face went a bit red and he started pulling at one of his ears and I had to bite the inside of my cheek to stop myself from laughing!

Acknowledgements

A huge, huggy THANK YOU to my brilliant editor,
Kirsty, and my amazing agent, Becky,
for all their support and friendship.

Thanks also to EVERYONE at Nosy Crow
and the British Museum who worked with me
on this book – it was loads of fun!

Huge thanks to the super-talented Tom for
the fantastic illustrations. I hope that you and
I will be writing about and illustrating
toga-wearing-ferrets for the rest of our lives.

And thank you to Albie's daddy, Andy,
for his support while I wrote this book.
And to Albie for being my baby Antimachus.

Zeus4eva.

The Police AND the Fire Brigade

For once in my life I wish my mum would understand just how DANGEROUS it is at my school and not say things to me like, "Stop telling tales" or "Don't EXAGGERATE, Izzy" or "Are you SURE the police AND the fire brigade had to come?"

Zach (that's my friend) says that our school is a

DISASTER ZONE

and I think he's right because that's EXACTLY what the fireman said when Gary Petrie got stuck inside the recycling bins again.

And one time after the whole DEMON DINNER LADIES thing, our friend Maisie actually filled in an application to transfer to another school and we had to stop her from posting it because we wanted her to stay with us and also because Jodi says there is

STRENGTH IN NUMBERS (which means it's better to have four of us and not three of us when all the weird stuff starts happening and we have to save the whole school).

But one of the WORST things that's ever happened to us was when it started snowing and it wouldn't stop.

Zach says that we should have DEFINITELY STAYED INDOORS when we heard the

WEIRD
WAILING SOUND

in the playground. And he was right because

if we had then Maisie probably wouldn't have been swept away by the TORNADO.

And even though all the teachers kept telling us that everything was COMPLETELY FINE we all knew that it was COMPLETELY NOT FINE. And in fact that it was probably the most COMPLETELY OPPOSITE OF FINE that you can get because we knew that there was a BEAST on the way to our school.

And we had NO IDEA how to stop it!

Snow Day

Loads of stuff stresses my mum out. Like when she's making tea and I need to be in the kitchen looking for my swimming goggles. Or when Gran says, "When was the last time you dusted in here?" Or when my dad uses the toilet for almost an hour when Mum has guests coming.

But the thing that stresses my mum out the MOST is when it starts snowing. And last week as soon as she saw a TINY SPECK of snow she started

FREAKING OUT

and trying to phone the school and she kept pacing up and down the hall saying, "Come on. Answer. Answer. ANSWER!" And I had to shout that I was TRYING TO SLEEP ACTUALLY because it was 7.23am and I do not have to get up until 7.30am.

And that's when someone started
BANGING on our front door and Mum
shouted, "Izzy! You'll have to get that. I'm
on the phone!"

So I got up and I was sure that it must be
some sort of

SERIOUS EMERGENCY

because I didn't know who would be
banging on the door as loud or as **MUCH** as
that at 7.23am except for a police officer or
a fire fighter or maybe the Queen. But when
I opened the door I saw that it wasn't any

of those people because it was Zach's mum who lives in the flat below us.

At first I thought there was maybe something wrong with Zach or his cat or something because Zach's mum looked PANICKED.

But then she said, "Do we know yet? DO WE KNOW?!"